Frog and Toad All Year

by Arnold Lobel

An I CAN READ Book

SCHOLASTIC INC.

New York Toronto London Auckland Sydney
Mexico City New Delhi Hong Kong Buenos Aires

To James Marshall

A portion of this book previously appeared in *Cricket*.

ISBN 0-439-43190-5

12 11 10 9 8 7 6 5 4 3 2   2 3 4 5 6 7/0

Printed in the U.S.A.   23

First Scholastic printing, September 2002

Contents

Down the Hill

Frog knocked at Toad's door.
"Toad, wake up," he cried.
"Come out and see
how wonderful the winter is!"

"I will not," said Toad.
"I am in my warm bed."

"Winter is beautiful,"
said Frog.
"Come out and have fun."

"Blah," said Toad.
"I do not have
any winter clothes."

Frog came into the house.
"I have brought you
some things to wear," he said.
Frog pushed a coat
down over the top of Toad.
Frog pulled snowpants
up over the bottom of Toad.

He put a hat and scarf
on Toad's head.

"Help!" cried Toad.
"My best friend
is trying to kill me!"

"I am only getting you ready
for winter," said Frog.

Frog and Toad went outside.
They tramped through the snow.
"We will ride
down this big hill
on my sled," said Frog.

"Not me," said Toad.

"Do not be afraid," said Frog.
"I will be with you
on the sled.
It will be a fine, fast ride.
Toad, you sit in front.
I will sit right behind you."

The sled began to move
down the hill.
"Here we go!"
said Frog.

There was a bump.
Frog fell off the sled.
Toad rushed past trees and rocks.
"Frog, I am glad
that you are here," said Toad.

Toad leaped over
a snowbank.

"I could not steer the sled
without you, Frog," he said.
"You are right. Winter is fun!"

A crow flew nearby.
"Hello Crow," shouted Toad.
"Look at Frog and me.
We can ride a sled
better than anybody
in the world!"

"But Toad," said the crow,
"you are alone on the sled."

Toad looked around.
He saw that Frog was not there.
"I AM ALL ALONE!"
screamed Toad.

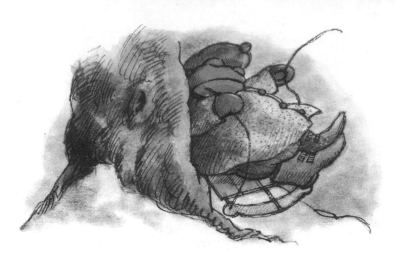

Bang!

The sled hit a tree.

Thud!

The sled hit a rock.

Plop!
The sled dived
into the snow.

Frog came running down the hill.
He pulled Toad out of the snow.
"I saw everything," said Frog.
"You did very well
by yourself."

"I did not," said Toad.
"But there is one thing
that I can do
all by myself."

"What is that?" asked Frog.

"I can go home," said Toad.
"Winter may be beautiful,
but bed is much better."

The Corner

Frog and Toad
were caught in the rain.
They ran to Frog's house.
"I am all wet," said Toad.
"The day is spoiled."

"Have some tea and cake,"
said Frog. "The rain will stop.
If you stand near the stove,
your clothes will soon be dry.

I will tell you a story
while we are waiting," said Frog.

"Oh good," said Toad.

"When I was small,
not much bigger
than a pollywog," said Frog,
"my father said to me,
'Son, this is a cold, gray day
but spring
is just around the corner.'

I wanted spring to come.
I went out
to find that corner.
I walked down a path in the woods
until I came to a corner.
I went around the corner
to see if spring
was on the other side."

"And was it?" asked Toad.

"No," said Frog.
"There was only a pine tree,
three pebbles
and some dry grass.

I walked
in the meadow.
Soon I came to
another corner.
I went around the corner
to see if spring was there."

"Did you find it?" asked Toad.

"No," said Frog.
"There was only
an old worm
asleep on a
tree stump."

"I walked along the river
until I came to
another corner.
I went around the corner
to look for spring."

"Was it there?" asked Toad.

"No," said Frog.

"There was only
some wet mud
and a lizard who was chasing
his tail."

"You must have been tired,"
said Toad.

"I was tired," said Frog,
"and it started
to rain."

"I went back home.
When I got there," said Frog,
"I found another corner.
It was the corner of my house."

"Did you go around it?"
asked Toad.

"I went around that corner, too,"
said Frog.

"What did you see?"
asked Toad.

"I saw the sun coming out,"
said Frog. "I saw birds
sitting and singing in a tree.
I saw my mother and father
working in their garden.
I saw flowers in the garden."

"You found it!" cried Toad.

"Yes," said Frog.
"I was very happy.
I had found the corner
that spring was just around."

"Look, Frog," said Toad.
"You were right.
The rain has stopped."
Frog and Toad hurried outside.

They ran around the corner
of Frog's house
to make sure
that spring had come again.

Ice Cream

One hot summer day
Frog and Toad sat by the pond.
"I wish we had some
sweet, cold ice cream," said Frog.

"What a good idea," said Toad.
"Wait right here, Frog.
I will be back soon."
Toad went to the store.
He bought two big ice-cream cones.

Toad licked one of the cones.
"Frog likes chocolate best,"
said Toad, "and so do I."

Toad walked along the path.
A large, soft drop
of chocolate ice cream
slipped down his arm.
"This ice cream
is melting in the sun,"
said Toad.

Toad walked faster.
Many drops
of melting ice cream
flew through the air.
They fell down on Toad's head.
"I must hurry back
to Frog!" he cried.

More and more
of the ice cream
was melting.
It dripped down
on Toad's jacket.
It splattered
on his pants
and on his feet.

"Where is the path?"
cried Toad.
"I cannot see!"

Frog sat by the pond
waiting for Toad.
A mouse ran by.

"I just saw something awful!"
cried the mouse.
"It was big and brown!"

"Something covered
with sticks and leaves is moving
this way!" cried a squirrel.

"Here comes a thing with horns!"
shouted a rabbit.
"Run for your life!"

"What can it be?" asked Frog.

Frog hid behind a rock.
He saw the thing coming.
It was big and brown.
It was covered
with sticks and leaves.
It had two horns.

"Frog," cried the thing.
"Where are you?"

"Good heavens!"
said Frog.
"That thing is Toad!"

Toad fell into the pond.
He sank to the bottom
and came up again.
"Drat," said Toad.
"All of our sweet, cold ice cream
has washed away."

"Never mind," said Frog.
"I know what we can do."
Frog and Toad quickly ran back
to the store.
Then they sat in the shade
of a large tree
and ate
their chocolate
ice-cream cones
together.

The Surprise

It was October.
The leaves had fallen off
the trees.
They were lying on the ground.
"I will go to Toad's house,"
said Frog.
"I will rake all of the leaves
that have fallen on his lawn.
Toad will be surprised."

Frog took a rake
out of the
garden shed.

Toad looked out of his window.
"These messy leaves
have covered everything," said Toad.
He took a rake out of the closet.
"I will run over to Frog's house.
I will rake all of his leaves.
Frog will be very pleased."

Frog ran through the woods
so that Toad would not see him.

Toad ran through the high grass
so that Frog would not see him.

Frog came to Toad's house.
He looked in the window.

"Good," said Frog.
"Toad is out.
He will never know
who raked his leaves."

Toad got to Frog's house.
He looked in the window.
"Good," said Toad.
"Frog is not home.
He will never guess
who raked his leaves."

Frog worked hard.
He raked the leaves into a pile.
Soon Toad's lawn was clean.
Frog picked up his rake
and started home.

Toad pushed and pulled on the rake.
He raked the leaves into a pile.
Soon there was not a single leaf
in Frog's front yard.
Toad took his rake
and started home.

A wind came.
It blew across the land.
The pile of leaves
that Frog had raked for Toad
blew everywhere.
The pile of leaves
that Toad had raked for Frog
blew everywhere.

When Frog got home,
he said, "Tomorrow I will
clean up the leaves
that are all over my own lawn.
How surprised Toad must be!"

When Toad got home,
he said, "Tomorrow I will
get to work and rake
all of my own leaves.
How surprised Frog must be!"

That night
Frog and Toad
were both happy
when they each
turned out the light
and went to bed.

Christmas Eve

On Christmas Eve
Toad cooked a big dinner.
He decorated the tree.

"Frog is late," said Toad.
Toad looked at his clock.
He remembered it was broken.
The hands of the clock did not move.
Toad opened the front door.
He looked out into the night.

Frog was not there.
"I am worried,"
said Toad.

"What if something terrible
has happened?" said Toad.
"What if Frog has fallen
into a deep hole
and cannot get out?
I will never see him again!"

Toad opened the door once more.
Frog was not on the path.

"What if Frog is lost
in the woods?"
said Toad.
"What if
he is cold
and wet
and hungry?"

"What if Frog is being chased
by a big animal
with many sharp teeth?
What if he is being eaten up?"
cried Toad.
"My friend and I
will never have
another Christmas together!"

Toad found some rope in the cellar.
"I will pull Frog out of the hole
with this," said Toad.

Toad found a lantern in the attic.
"Frog will see this light.
I will show him the way
out of the woods," said Toad.

Toad found a frying pan
in the kitchen.
"I will hit that big animal
with this," said Toad.
"All of his teeth
will fall out.
Frog, do not worry," cried Toad.
"I am coming to help you!"

Toad ran out
of his house.

There was Frog.

"Hello, Toad," he said.
"I am very sorry to be late.
I was wrapping your present."

"You are not at the bottom
of a hole?" asked Toad.

"No," said Frog.

"You are not lost
in the woods?" asked Toad.

"No," said Frog.

"You are not being eaten
by a big animal?"
asked Toad.

"No," said Frog. "Not at all."

"Oh, Frog," said Toad,
"I am so glad to be
spending Christmas with you."

Toad opened his present from Frog.
It was a beautiful new clock.
The two friends sat by the fire.
The hands of the clock
moved to show the hours
of a merry Christmas Eve.